A Simple Idea to Empower KIds based on the power of love, choice and belief

by Kathleen Boucher

Balboa Press books may be ordered through booksellers or by contacting:

Balboa Press
A Division of Hay House
1663 Liberty Drive
Bloomington, IN 47403
www.balboapress.com
1 (877) 407-4847

Because of the dynamic nature of the Internet, any web addresses or links contained in this book may have changed since publication and may no longer be valid. The views expressed in this work are solely those of the author and do not necessarily reflect the views of the publisher, and the publisher hereby disclaims any responsibility for them.

Any people depicted in stock imagery provided by Thinkstock are models, and such images are being used for illustrative purposes only.
Certain stock imagery © Thinkstock.

ISBN: 978-1-4525-9142-1 (sc)
ISBN: 978-1-4525-9143-8 (e)

Library of Congress Control Number: 2014901713

Printed in the United States of America.

Balboa Press rev. date: 01/28/2014

BALBOA.
PRESS
A DIVISION OF HAY HOUSE

A Simple Idea
to Empower Kids

Based on the Power of Love,
Choice, and Belief

by

Kathleen Boucher

Stop for a minute and listen. Do you hear that?
It is your heart beating. It is filled with love.
Love is the greatest force on Earth.

Can you keep a secret? Promise me you won't tell? From the beginning of time until the end of time there will only be one of you on Earth. Only one! This means you are very special exactly as you are right now.

It does not matter what you look like on the outside. All that matters is what you believe. Words can never hurt you unless you give them permission to.

Hurtful words roll right off of you. They are slippery and land on the floor. Throw them away. Believe in yourself. Believe in your heart. It is filled with love.

Can you keep a secret? Yes, another one! The second greatest force on Earth is the power to choose. Wow! You get to choose your thoughts.

Thoughts have power. They become things. What do you want to do? What do you want to have? What do you want to be? I want you to promise me you will dream BIG!

When you go to bed tonight close your eyes and see in your head what you want. Believe you already have it. Make believe! When you wake up say "Thank you, thank you, thank you!"

Know in your heart you can do it. Know in your heart you can have it. Know in your heart you can be it. Remember I told you your heart is where love is.

Love is the greatest force on Earth. From the beginning of time until the end of time there will only be one of you. You are very, very special. The World needs you.

Are you ready for one more secret? I promise you this is the last one. Believe you can do it. Think about it as many times as you want to every day! Then think about it some more. Be happy!

Send this happiness around the World three times. Laugh out loud! Tell your best friend. Smile. Dream big. You are perfect just the way you are! The World needs you.

This book is dedicated to my brilliant husband Brian and my two amazing children, Christian and Michelle.

A Simple Idea to Empower Kids based on love, choice and belief

By Kathleen Boucher

CPSIA information can be obtained at www.ICGtesting.com
Printed in the USA
BVOW10s0033090414

350119BV00003B/21/P